THE UNBROKEN HEARTS CLUB

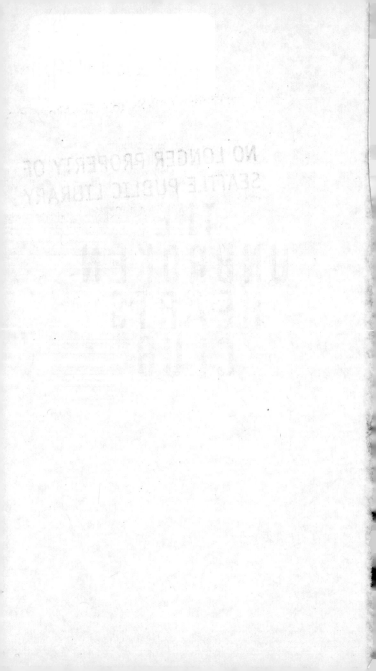

THE UNBROKEN HEARTS CLUB

Brooke Carter

orca soundings

ORCA BOOK PUBLISHERS

Library and Archives Canada Cataloguing in Publication

Carter, Brooke, 1977–, author
The unbroken hearts club / Brooke Carter.
(Orca soundings)

Issued in print and electronic formats.
ISBN 978-1-4598-2061-6 (softcover).—ISBN 978-1-4598-2062-3 (PDF).—
ISBN 978-1-4598-2063-0 (EPUB)

I. Title. II. Series: Orca soundings
PS8605.A77776U53 2019   jC813'.6   C2018-904888-3
                                                C2018-904889-1

First published in the United States, 2019
Library of Congress Control Number: 2018954089

Summary: In this high-interest novel for teen readers, Logan uses her camera to work through the grief of losing her mother.

MIX
Paper from
responsible sources
FSC® C016245

Orca Book Publishers is dedicated to preserving the environment and has printed this book on Forest Stewardship Council® certified paper.

Orca Book Publishers gratefully acknowledges the support for its publishing programs provided by the following agencies: the Government of Canada, the Canada Council for the Arts and the Province of British Columbia through the BC Arts Council and the Book Publishing Tax Credit.

Edited by Tanya Trafford
Cover images by iStock.com/Mny-Jhee (front) and
Shutterstock.com/Krasovski Dmitri (back)

ORCA BOOK PUBLISHERS
orcabook.com

Printed and bound in Canada.

22 21 20 19 • 4 3 2 1

For my mom

Chapter One

Snapshot of your morning, Logan. Mom's voice hums in my mind, like a radio turned way down low. Or someone calling from underwater. Where is she now? Is she in the air? Is she in the river I photographed this morning? Maybe she is in the other room. Maybe she's nowhere.

On days like today, when I'm in my darkroom, I feel like the answer is nowhere. I have to push the creeping feeling of panic all the way down so all that's left is…a numb, gray nothing. I push it down until I'm nothing and nowhere too.

But okay, Mom, here's a snapshot of my morning. I woke before dawn, gathered my trusty manual Pentax camera and a couple of rolls of black-and-white film. I snuck out of my basement bedroom window to take some shots at the riverbank on the edge of town.

The river was Mom's favorite place. Dad had the memorial bench installed. I didn't have to sneak out—I doubt Dad cares that I've been getting up early for a change—but if he knew where I've been going, he'd try to tag along. I don't have time for that. Dad is the opposite of me. He's all raw feelings and big dramatic gestures. He always wants to talk, talk, talk. He will talk about Mom to anyone who will listen, even strangers in the grocery store.

That's why Dad loves his grief support group so much. All they do is sit around and talk about the people they've lost. Mom died of Huntington's disease, which is an evil genetic disorder that is 100 percent fatal. As in, there's no cure. Just suffering. Dad wants to talk and I do my best not to. I want to be left alone in my darkroom. In here, all that exists are the photographs. Snapshots of time. There's no death.

I've been getting up before the sun to take photos—I need the magical morning light to capture the image I've been seeking, and that special lighting doesn't last long. It's beautiful for a few minutes, then gorgeous for a moment, and then it's back to being regular boring daylight.

That's when I come back to my darkroom to develop my shots. I know where every basin, canister and clothespin is by feel in here. My trusty tongs—the red silicone ones with a tomato on the handle that I stole from Dad's barbecue set—are always hanging on a nail at my workbench. I can hook them with my finger and wield them like a magic wand, bringing images into existence. When the lights are on, you can see all the images from my favorite photographers and filmmakers. I have cut and pasted them together to create a kind of wallpaper collage.

Cole will be here at any second to try and convince me to go to school. We've been best friends for our entire lives. Unlike me, he never seems to worry about anything. It's his main talent, apart from being a great filmmaker.

I gently swish the paper in the chemicals as the first image appears. This is my favorite part—seeing the picture appear out of nothing. Now I can see the riverbank and the bench. There is no one in the photo. Of course there isn't. There wasn't anyone there to begin with. And yet each time I develop one of these shots, some part of me expects to see my mom's long dark hair and slight frame perched on the bench.

Some people are intimidated by film processing, but I find it easy. Of course, there's an art to it. But that art is threatening to become extinct since everyone now shoots in digital. I use a digital SLR app for the camera on my phone too, but for me the true art of photography is about the complex relationship between light and film.

Despite Dad complaining that soon he'll have no place for his fishing equipment, I converted the large storage closet under the stairs into my darkroom. It's next to the rec room where

Cole and I hang out and have our movie nights. I've got all the different materials and chemicals I need in here. To avoid light contamination, I sealed off the entry with an extra folding door inside the original one. It's my own personal sanctuary.

The trick to developing film is that you have to keep it in total darkness until the end of the process. This suits me fine. Living in total darkness is kind of my thing. If it wasn't for Cole showing up every morning to drag me to school with him, I'd probably never interact with another human. Apart from my dad.

Thinking about Cole is complicated. I mean, he's my best friend for sure, but he's restless. He wants more from me than I can give. It's flattering, but I don't have anything left over for anyone else.

Ever since Mom died, it's like the light meter of life got turned way down to low. Colors are washed out, sounds are muffled, and my feelings—even feelings for guys—are blank. The girls at school can't understand it. I mean, Cole is hot, and not just hot for our small town. He's big-city hot, movie-star hot. Put-his-poster-on-your-wall-and-make-out-with-it hot. Drive-by-his-house-hoping-to-catch-a-glimpse-of-him hot. Leave-him-secret-love-notes hot. You get the idea. He's like a modern-day Paul Newman. Cole would pass out with joy if I ever said that to him (Luke from *Cool Hand Luke* is his blueprint for manhood). Why am I able to resist the irresistible? Why can't I return the feelings he has for me?

Forget it. I don't want to think about it now. As I clip up the prints, I see that I haven't captured the images quite the way I wanted to. Some parts are underexposed, and the compositions seem a little boring. I'll have to try again tomorrow.

I don't know what I'm looking for in these photos. It's not the trees, the leaves or the returning of the birds to the river. It's the empty spaces and the places I can't see. What's behind the large tree in the foreground? What's under the surface of the water?

I can't help feeling like there's something there, something I need, something waiting.

Right on cue I hear Cole's boots stomping down the stairs. And, as usual, he doesn't knock on my darkroom door. He opens the outer threshold a crack.

"Lo?" he whispers.

I sigh. "Cole. Film is not sound sensitive. It's light sensitive."

"Whatever," he says. "You done? Can I?"

"Yeah, yeah," I say, pulling open the inner door and switching on the regular light bulb.

Cole's sandy blond scruff of hair comes into the light from the shadows. He gives his head a little shake to get his bangs out of his pale blue eyes. He's smiling at me, his usual everything-is-right-with-the-world smile. I feel... nothing. I fake a smile in return and see a strange expression flicker across his face for a moment.

Cole looks at the photos drying on the line overhead.

"More bench, huh?" he says. "Lolo, when are you going to stop with all these very sad photos of the saddest bench in the history of benches?"

Cole is the one human being on earth who can call me Lolo without being murdered. That's because he's been my best friend since I moved in across the street when we were both two.

(He couldn't say my full name, Logan Imogen Flanagan, so he called me Lolo.) Now he mostly calls me Lo, since we're not babies anymore. But he does reserve the Lolo for when he's trying to sweet-talk me. I guess I kind of like it, though these days it's tough to figure out just what I like and what I don't like.

By the way, my middle name comes from my mom's all-time favorite photographer.

Here is a snapshot. Imogen Cunningham was a photographer who was famous for taking soft-focus, blurred images of her subjects. Later on she created a sharp-focus style of photography that led to the formation of Group f/64—a bunch of photographers all obsessed with the same technique. Imogen Cunningham was pretty badass, considering she was born in the late 1800s.

My mom was a photographer too, and she took a lot of photos in the Cunningham style. They were some of the best shots I've ever seen, even though she never shared them with anyone else.

My first name, Logan, well, that's 100 percent my dad. Yep, I'm named after his favorite comic book character, Wolverine. Dad is a huge comic book nerd, although he hasn't been reading them much lately. He hasn't been doing much at all besides going to work, trudging through the day and going to his support group. Dead wives will have that effect on you, I guess.

"Lo?" Cole bumps my shoulder a little too hard. I look up at him.

When did he get so solid and... muscular?

"Sorry—don't know my own strength," he says.

"Are you growing again, Cole?" I ask. "Weren't you, like, two inches shorter yesterday?"

"Yeah, probably," he says, and starts telling me about his breakfast as I pack up my camera and grab my backpack. "I woke up today and ate two eggs over easy, plus toast and juice. But then I had to have some raisin bran. And for some reason that made me hungry for cheese, so I made two toasted cheese sandwiches and grabbed an apple on my way out the door. My mom says I'm going to eat us out of house and home…" He trails off and looks sad.

This is another worst thing in a thousand worst things that happen when your mom dies—people feel like they can't talk about their own moms. And it's true. You don't really want them to.

He changes the subject. Cole is nothing if not dialed into my feelings, or lack thereof. "We should get going. We'll be late for Media Arts."

"Ugh, crap." You'd think Media Arts would be a good subject for me, right? Wrong. I'm close to flunking.

"Logan Imogen Flanagan." Cole cocks his head at me and narrows his eyes.

"Don't start," I say, but it's too late. He's on to me.

"You didn't do the assignment again, did you?" His voice takes on a shrill scolding tone. I can tell he's trying to make me laugh.

I feel bad because it's not working. I throw my hands up in silent surrender and hope he'll leave it at that.

"Fine," he says. "Get your butt in the car. We'd better get to school if you have a hope in hell of graduating with me."

"Lead on, captain," I say. But I'm dreading it.

We leave my darkroom and turn the corner to head up the steps. The last thing I see is the large family portrait hanging above the rec room fireplace. Snapshot: Mom, Dad, Daughter. Smiling in the sun. Spring flowers. An explosion of bright color. Blossoms on the trees. The promise of the future. Last known photo of Family Flanagan. A technicolor reminder of all we've lost.

Chapter Two

I open my locker and grab my Media Arts notebook. Cole waits beside me, fidgeting. People walk by and say hello. Girls check him out. Cole fits into the scenery like a famous actor hired to make the school more glamorous. He's at home in all habitats.

I'm dragging my feet. Today each student is supposed to discuss the progress of their yearlong project. I have nothing to show because I haven't even started. It's way past midterm. Everyone's already getting amped up for graduation and the looming end-of-the-year hullaballoo, to borrow an expression from Dad.

"I don't know why everyone is so excited about leaving high school," I mutter. Of course Cole hears me. He has hearing like a bat. Or maybe he always knows what I'm thinking. That's a possibility too.

"Because normal people look forward to the future, Lo. They don't waste their talent taking photos of sad benches." He arches an eyebrow at me.

I give him "the eyes" in response. This is a move in which yours truly makes her big brown eyes even more huge in her big moony face. My super-short pixie cut adds to the effect. When Cole first saw it, he declared it the greatest haircut I've ever had. He called me Winona Ryder for weeks.

He looks at me now and takes a small step back, leaning into the lockers like he's been sapped of all his strength.

"Oh no," he says. "Don't you dare, Lo. I'm trying to talk some sense into you. But you know I can't resist 'the eyes.'" He slithers down the bank of lockers and falls into a heap on the linoleum.

"You should be an actor instead of a director," I say, slamming my locker shut. "Because that performance was sneeze-worthy."

Cole springs up to standing. "You did not just reference the single greatest acting moment in cinema history."

"I did," I say, turning toward class.

"You do realize that the Keanu Reeves sneeze in *The Lake House* will go down as the benchmark by which all future acting generations measure their work?"

During one of our many epic movie-watching nights, Cole and I discovered this cinema gem. It's kind of our thing.

"Uh-huh," I say. "And Keanu's not bad to look at."

"Lo, he's, like, three times your age!"

"What can I say? I like them…old and dark and handsome." This is a total lie, but it's fun to torture Cole.

"You're killing me, Lo. Killing me."

"I aim to please," I say, pausing at the Media Arts room door.

"After you," says Cole.

I give him the eyes again, and he nudges me through the door.

Twenty minutes into class, Cole reaches over and grabs my wrist, placing his fingers on my pulse. He does this some-times—it's his dramatic way of seeing if I'm checked in or checked out. Right now I'm checked out. The updates are so boring, I can't keep my eyes open.

When Ms. Mill calls on me to give my update, I shrug.

"See me after class, Logan," she says. I know I'm doomed.

I try my best to pay attention during the rest of class, but my mind keeps wandering. I can't stop staring out the window. I see the trees and I think about the riverbank down the street.

"Hey," says the girl next to me. Her name is Cheryl, or Sherry—I can never get it straight. "What's with you guys?" she asks, nodding toward Cole.

"Huh?" I play dumb, but I know what she means. Everyone always wants to know if we're a couple.

"He's *fiiine*," she says, drawing the word out.

"Yeah, and quite the sneezer too," I answer.

She gives me a blank look, and we stare at each other for a moment.

Cole clears his throat. He heard the entire exchange. "This is why you don't have any friends, Lo," he says.

"I have you," I say, turning to look at him.

"Yeah," he says. "You do." He looks at me with such intensity that I have to look away.

It's a relief when class is over. I need a break. I'm almost out the door when Ms. Mill stops me.

"Logan," she says. "I'm not going to say the same old thing again, because we've had this conversation a few times now."

I nod.

"This is a note that you need to show your father," she says, handing me a piece of paper. "Please have him sign it and return it to me."

I open it. It's a note, all right. It spells out all the ways I am screwing up my chances of graduating.

"Start your project, Logan. Pick something. Please," says Ms. Mill.

"Okay," I manage. I turn to leave.

"And Logan," she adds. "I'm…here if you need me."

I pause at the doorway. My brain tells me to turn around, give the poor woman a smile, tell her I'll be fine. But my heart won't let me. I manage a slight nod and get out of there as fast as I can.

As usual, the rest of the day is a blur of meaningless high school drudgery. Classes that I don't need, free study time I won't use, a pointless lunch break (I didn't pack a lunch and wouldn't eat much anyway). I have no time for the social experiment of high school.

I end up skipping last period to sit under the big maple trees out front and photograph the leaves as they fall. It gives me something to do while I wait for Cole to be finished.

After the last bell, he finds me under the trees and plunks onto the grass, close to me. He props himself up on an elbow. I take his photo, the sunlight filtering through the leaves and dancing across his face. Having my camera between us feels safer.

"So how's my favorite nihilist?" he asks.

"I'm not a nihilist," I say. "Do you even know what that word means?"

He looks wounded. "Hey, I read a philosophy book once. You know, staring into the abyss and all that."

"Ha."

"Plus," he adds, "I've seen *The Big Lebowski* at least a hundred times."

"Well, that is as good as an advanced philosophy degree for sure."

He chuckles and then grows serious. "What do I have to do to get you to laugh, Lo?" he asks. "I miss your laugh."

"Don't try," I say. "Just be here. Okay?"

"Okay," he says gently. "Did Ms. Mill come down on you very hard?"

I toss him the letter, Cole opens it.

"Uh-oh. Daddy Flanagan's not going to like this one," he says.

"Will you come back to the house with me?" I ask, giving him the eyes again.

Cole groans. "Yeah, yeah," he says. "Besides, we were supposed to watch *Dog Day Afternoon* again, right?" As is typical for young aspiring male film-makers, Cole is going through a real Al Pacino phase. Again. I much prefer his Tarantino phase, but whatever.

"Fine," I say, "but don't start screaming about *Attica* again. It's irritating."

He tosses a handful of leaves at me and I let them fall on me, not bothering to brush them away.

"Come on," he says, pulling me up.

We go find his beater car. As usual it's parked in the staff parking lot, and as usual Cole gets away with breaking the rules.

When we get to my house, Dad's not home from work yet, so I leave the letter on the kitchen table.

Cole and I retreat to the basement to watch movies, and I find myself daydreaming. I can't stop thinking about being under the trees with Cole. With him next to me like that, so close, I felt something. For a long time I've been worried that I'm broken or defective. But today I felt the energy of his long body next to mine. It was like my nerve endings sparked to life for a second before snuffing out again.

"Lo?" Cole asks, watching my face. "You okay?"

I had been staring at him. I look away.

"Snapshot," Cole says. I give him a dirty look.

"Snapshot," he repeats, knowing full well that this is his trump card.

I take a breath. "I feel…" I trail off, unsure what to say.

Cole scoots a little closer on the big sectional couch, his long arm snaking behind me. He's close enough that I can smell him. He smells good.

"Go on," he says.

"I'm not sure," I say. "I have these feelings, sort of. Sometimes. But it's like they're buried. And I don't know how to dig them up."

"I have feelings I don't know what to do with too," he says with a grin.

I look up at him, at his soft blue eyes. How messed up am I? There's another Logan inside me, I know it. And she is falling in love with her best friend. But this new, broken Logan has taken over, and she says no.

He leans toward me, and oh my god, he's going to try to kiss me. But before he can follow through, before I can stop him or kiss him first or run away or smack him or dump my Dr. Pepper in his lap, I hear a chair scrape on the kitchen floor overhead.

"LOGAN!" Dad yells from the kitchen. He's home. He has read the letter.

Cole sits upright and moves away. Moment ruined. *Phew*.

Chapter Three

Cole watches, eating tortilla chips by the handful, as Dad paces in front of me. I had expected Dad to start yelling when he came downstairs, but he's been silent so far. Like he's not sure what to say. I know he doesn't want to be mean to me, not now. I hate that I'm making him worry about me on top of everything.

"Look, honey," he says. "I'm not going to say enough is enough. I can't say that for you. Grief is personal."

Here he goes again with his support-group talk. I already did the therapy thing, and it didn't help. Then the doctor prescribed medication that made my lack of feelings even more lacking. I wasn't human, and I hated it. I'm only sort of human now.

"But," he continues, "it has been a year since Mom died—"

"Not quite a year yet," I say.

Dad sighs. "No, not yet. Almost. And she was sick for so long. But the point is, Logan, it's time to make some changes. I want to make some changes."

"Like what?" I ask, starting to get worried. "We're not going to move or something, are we?"

"No! No," he says. "It's…" He trails off, running his fingers through his thick dark hair. He does have such great hair—so much better than most guys his age. It's not even receding or anything. I suppose that once upon a time he was even considered handsome.

Cole starts to speak, mouth full of chips. I try to wave at him to shush, but as usual he ignores me. "Please don't come down too hard on her, Mr. F. She's trying. I see her trying."

Okay, now he's lying for me.

"And," he adds, "I'm helping her. Don't do anything rash, Mr. F. Like, don't take her darkroom away."

"What the hell, Cole?" I yell. What is he giving my dad ideas for?

Cole cringes. "Yeesh, sorry, Lo. I didn't mean—that was dumb."

"Well," says Dad, "that is something I wanted to talk to you about."

"Oh my god, what? You're not going to take away my darkroom, are you?" I'm starting to panic now. I'll have nothing to live for.

"No, but I'm, uh, I'm going to need to use this space. Not the darkroom, honey, not that. The basement."

"You mean our viewing theater, Mr. F.?" Cole asks, back to munching. His hunger is clearly not affected by parental doom.

Dad rubs his temples. "Cole, isn't it getting close to dinnertime?"

Cole shrugs.

Dad sits down next to me and takes my hand. "I need the basement, honey, because I'm going to start hosting my support group here. The current organizer, Kelsey—you met her at the barbecue last summer, remember?— well, she's making some big changes in her career and doesn't have the time and space to host it anymore—"

"Wait. You want to have your meetings here? In this house? In my basement?"

My dad nods.

"As in, the place I go to escape the misery of human existence and contemplate the meaninglessness of the universe?"

Dad sighs a sigh so deep it seems to come from his feet. "Wow," he says. "For a second there I forgot how over-dramatic teenagers can be."

I scowl at him in return. I know I'm being difficult.

"Wait," says Cole, opening his big mouth again. "Isn't that Kelsey lady the one who made the rad chicken wings?"

Of course that's how Cole would remember someone.

Dad chuckles and nods. And is it my imagination or is he blushing a little? What is happening?

"Nice," says Cole.

Dad looks at me and squeezes my hand. "I need this, honey."

"Whatever," I manage. "If it helps you, then fine."

"Good," says Dad, hopping up. "Because it starts tonight, and everyone will be here in an hour." He turns to go back upstairs.

"*Tonight?*" I ask.

"Yep," Dad says. "And you two are in charge of refreshments."

"But Dad!" I protest.

He holds up the letter. "You will help with the group meetings. All of them, no exceptions. In return, I will sign the letter. You will also finish your Media Arts project—on time. Or I *will* be finding another use for that darkroom."

"Damn," Cole whispers. "Stone cold, Mr. F."

"Understood?" Dad asks.

"Understood," I say.

Cole gives him a salute, and Dad marches back upstairs.

I give Cole a death stare, but he grins back at me. It's impossible to stay mad at him. I flop back onto the couch.

"Well, who knows?" Cole says. "This group thing could be a real hoot."

"Cole, it's a bunch of sad people talking about how awful life is. How can that be fun? You remember that horrible barbecue at the lake."

"I don't know," he says, snuggling next to me. He still smells good. "We could make some guac, spike the punch, inject some life into this weird death group."

"Do me a favor?" I ask.

"Anything."

"Don't ever say *guac* again."

Cole laughs. "Didn't you have a name for this group? I seem to remember some famous Logan Flanagan sarcasm on the topic."

"I called it the Broken Hearts Club."

"Yeah, that's it. Doesn't seem as clever now though. Seems kind of mean."

"Yeah," I say, too drained to banter anymore.

Cole stands up and hauls me off the couch by the arms. He's got his I-have-the-best-idea-ever face on.

"Oh no, what?" I ask.

"I have the best idea ever."

Something tells me I don't want to know what it is.

Chapter Four

Cole's idea is not that bad, considering the doozers he's had in the past. Like the time when we were ten and he tried to convince me we could parachute from his second-floor balcony. With bedsheets. He jumped. I didn't. He spent the summer in a full leg cast. And then there was the time he had the brilliant idea to spin donuts in a snowy parking lot—Cole = 0, lamppost = 1.

Cole's great idea this time was to help out cheerfully with the Broken Hearts Club while observing its members for artistic inspiration. He could get footage to use for his project. And I might get some photos for my project, whatever that might be. Not to mention yummy snacks.

While he's outlining his grand plan, he is halving and scooping the avocados for the guacamole. Of course, he is referring to it as "guac" the entire time.

"But Cole," I say, "this is a group for sad people. Do you really think they want to be filmed while they are talking about such personal things?"

"We'll let them know it's for school, and we won't record anything from their private conversations. I'll just interview some of them."

"I don't know," I say. "I like the idea of taking their photos if they're fine with it. But recording them seems invasive. I know I wouldn't want that."

"Whoa," says Cole. He is looking out the kitchen window. "Like, Keanu-level whoa."

Someone has just pulled up in a sleek silver SUV. Dad is in the driveway. A tall, pretty brunette gets out of the SUV and gives Dad a bright, warm smile. It's Kelsey from the barbecue. Dad gives her a big smile right back, and they hug. My heart lurches a little. There's this weird flush of happiness and pain before it dissolves into nothing again.

"Looks like your dad has a thing for hot-wings Kelsey," Cole says. He shoots a glance at me, his face tight.

"Well," I say, "he's been lonely for a long time."

Mom passed away last year, yes. But her death had been a long time coming.

When someone has Huntington's disease, their symptoms can start when they are young, like my age. Mom learned a few years after I was born that she had the disease. She was adopted, so she didn't know her genetic history. Would she have chosen to have children had she known? And Dad, well, he had to live with the knowledge of her impending death for years. He had to watch the love of his life drift away.

"Lolo?" Cole says. He reaches out to me and pulls me into a hug. I don't resist. "Do you need to get away?" he asks. "Because I will straight up put you in my car and take you somewhere. The drive-in? The mall? The moon?"

I shake my head, unable to talk. I'm not sure what will happen if I open my mouth. But I can sense a tidal wave of feelings waiting to wipe me out. I can't let that happen. I can't fall apart. Not now. Not yet.

The kitchen door opens, and Dad clears his throat.

Cole steps away. I look at Dad and his friend Kelsey. They're standing close together, the way people do when they like each other. Kelsey gives me a warm smile and offers her hand. I try to look at her face, at her eyes, but it's like I can't take her in all at once. I focus on her outstretched hand. I'm relieved to see that her nails are filed short, and they're clean. I'm glad Dad doesn't have a crush on someone with horrible fake nails. I know it's kind of insane that I'm focusing on this. I take her hand to shake it. I manage a wobbly smile.

She's wearing some kind of floral scent. Lavender maybe. Her shoes are tasteful pumps, and her clothes are unfussy and neat. She wears a cross-body bag, and I like that she's the hands-free type. I can only glance at her hair. It's long and dark and shiny. So much like my mom's hair that I have to fight the urge to reach out and touch it.

"Hi, Logan," she says. "I'm Kelsey. It's great to officially meet you. David talks about you all the time."

David. Not "your dad," but "David."

"Cool," I say. My throat feels tight.

Dad is an awkward kind of guy at the best of times, so he's pretty much himself. He stands there with his hands in his pockets.

Cole breaks the silence. "Hi, Kelsey. I'm Cole." He reaches out to shake her hand too. "We met at the barbecue. Righteous wings."

"Oh, Logan's boyfriend, right?" she asks.

I open my mouth to correct her, but Cole answers before I do. "Yep," he says, catching me, and Dad, by surprise. I stare at Cole—hard.

"So are the snacks ready, guys?" Dad asks. "The rest of the group will be arriving soon."

I nod like a zombie.

We help Dad and Kelsey arrange the furniture downstairs in a circle and set out the snacks.

"I hate to say this, guys," Cole announces, "but this kinda looks like the headquarters of a cult meeting." As usual, he manages to say exactly what I'm thinking.

Kelsey laughs out loud, this huge laugh that fills the room. The effect it has on my dad is too intimate for me to witness. He glows when he looks at her.

I find my voice after a second. "I agree. This is creepy."

"Okay," says Kelsey, "what do you guys suggest?"

"Well," I say, "one of the things I've never liked about going to groups is that they seem so…group-y."

Kelsey nods. "Okay. I get that. I don't like that either."

"Like, it should be more than a meeting. Something more fun," I say.

"So death plus fun," Cole says, eliciting another belly laugh from Kelsey.

"I don't know," Dad says, staying true to his stick-in-the-mud act.

"I'm with Logan on this one," Kelsey says, walking over to stand next to me. "What should we do, Logan?"

"Um, I think we should decorate," I say. "Like for a party."

There is a moment of stillness, and then everyone gets moving. We turn the furniture back to a more casual formation, dim the lights a little, put on some background music. Dad and Cole have a brief argument over '90s versus '70s music—Dad wins. We go with '70s. And we all vow that the next meeting will have better snacks. Pizza maybe. Death plus pizza.

The doorbell rings as people arrive. I've met most of them before.

Give me a snapshot, Logan. My mom's voice again, this time vibrating in my chest as I stand against the back wall and watch our rec room fill up with people. All these breathing people inhabiting my space, interacting and talking. They do what living people do. They talk, laugh, cry, eat and then repeat.

When Mom was alive but bedridden, I would come home from school and she would ask me for a snapshot of my day. *I wish I could have a snapshot of your future*, she'd say. Some days, when moods were high, I'd design a fantastic future for myself. I'd be a famous photographer, living it up in Paris, surrounded by artists and all the mysteries of the world. Sometimes Cole would be in these futures as my film-making sidekick. Mom loved to hear about us. She would ask if I would go to prom with Cole and what my dress might look like. I knew she wanted to go even farther into the future too. Who would I become? Would I have kids—her grandkids—of my own? So I indulged her. But even as I told her these stories, I knew I was lying to us both.

My future isn't flashbulb bright. It's gray and blurry, as if the fates chose the wrong shutter speed when they took the snapshot of my life.

Okay, Mom, here's a snapshot of the meeting. There's Dad and Kelsey, infatuated with one another. Kelsey's husband died of lymphoma and they had no children. Kelsey's some kind of big deal marketing exec. Totally out of Dad's league. There's me and my apparent boyfriend, who is charming the pants off everyone. There's an older man named Humphrey who is dressed in brown polyester from head to toe and who calls me "lovey" when I bring him a drink or a snack. There are the three lawyers, Jim, Jim and John. They all lost their wives to breast cancer. They all need to learn how to use an iron. There's a sweet, sad lady named Grace who is around Dad's age. She lost her son in an accident. She still wears a T-shirt with his face on it most days. These are the core members of the Broken Hearts Club—the regulars, the diehards, the never-quits, the always-sads. The best, and worst, thing about this meeting is that each person manages to catch my eye at some point. It's like looking into a mirror.

It isn't long before Cole charms his way into asking people a few questions on camera. I ask a few of them if I can take their photos. They all say yes, but I'm still worried they're doing it because they feel sorry for me. I decide to use my digital camera so I can show them the photos right away. Then they can tell me if they want them deleted. To my surprise, most of them ask if they can have a copy. I take their email addresses and phone numbers and promise to make them prints.

My favorite moment is when I take a picture of Humphrey sitting in our large brown fake-leather recliner. He's a sea of brown with a sweet floating face in an aura of fluorescent light.

I snap a few candid shots of Dad and Kelsey talking in the corner. It feels a lot like eavesdropping. When I look at the photos, of the moments captured in time, all I see is the happiness on my dad's face.

I take some shots of Cole as he works the room too. When I review these shots, I see that I lingered over his shoulders and arms. I should delete them.

Cole sidles up to me at the end of the meeting. "You going to upload the shots to your Instagram or use them in your project?"

"I'm going to use them," I say. "I have an idea for a kind of photo essay or mixed-media type of thing. Not sure yet, but it's something."

"Good for you," he says. "Anyway, you wouldn't want to ruin your Insta feed. It's all photos of benches so far, right?"

I shake my head. He's relentless with the teasing.

"So," I say.

"So?" he asks.

I give him a look. "Earlier?"

He grins at me. "What?"

"You know," I say.

"Nope."

"God, you're infuriating."

"I think you mean adorable," he says.

"Cole."

"Logan."

I take a breath. "Look, you're not my boyfriend."

His always-on smile falters for a second. "I know that," he says.

We look at each other in silence. Then I try to explain.

"It's just that—"

"It's okay," he says, cutting me off. "You don't have to."

"Cole." I want him to understand. It's not that I don't have feelings for him. It's that my feelings don't work.

"Forget it," he says. "I'm over it." In true Cole style, he's up the stairs before I can say anything.

Chapter Five

The next several Broken Hearts Club meetings are a success. Cole seems to have shrugged off the whole boyfriend/ girlfriend thing. Or, at least, he's keeping it to himself. He keeps busy by filming the group. I'm taking lots of photos and trying to find a way to tie them all together.

We've been taking our Dad-mandated hosting duties seriously. We have tried to incorporate themes, like pizza night, sushi night and even a drive-in movie night. That one was a bit of a bust because no one wanted to climb into the giant cardboard car Cole built.

Things seem to be going well for Dad and Kelsey. They have been getting together outside of the meetings too. So far Dad has not called them "dates," but I'm sure that's to spare me. I'm fine with it, though, even if it is a little intense having Kelsey around so much.

One afternoon I walk into the kitchen after school and Kelsey is sitting at our table with her back to the door. For a half second I think it's Mom, and when she turns around, it is all I can do not to run from the room. Sometimes I find myself wondering what Kelsey's skin feels like. I know that sounds twisted. I don't mean it in a weird way. I just kind of want to hold her hand for a little while.

Cole hasn't shared his video footage with me, which is unlike him. It seems like he's pulling away a little. He did have another great idea to help some of the Broken Hearts Club members with their problems. Cole's need to fix broken people is intense. It turns out that my fave member, Humphrey, has a long-lost daughter, so Cole is coming over today to see if we can help him find her.

When Cole meets me in the basement, he can't sit still. He keeps getting up and wandering the room. At one point he grabs a pen and starts stabbing a bowl of fake fruit with it.

"Did you eat a bag of coffee or something?" I ask. But he isn't in the mood for teasing.

Humphrey has given us permission to post his photo on social media, along with a message. We note when and where his daughter was born and her first name at the time. It was Zelda, which I think is fabulous. Humphrey and Zelda's mom had a brief affair when Humphrey was young. But then she disappeared with baby Zelda. We're hoping someone sees the post and can reconnect them.

"You know," I say as I finish uploading, "baby Zelda's got to be, like, sixty or something by now."

"Not a baby," Cole says in a faraway voice, his face sad.

"You okay?" I ask.

He takes a deep breath. I'm freaked out by how weird things are between us. He has never been this awkward. "I want to go to the spring dance and I want you to go with me. And not in an ironic, let's-go-as-friends-and-make-fun-of-all-the-eager-dancers kind of way. In a sincere way. As in for real."

I stare at him, caught off guard. "You want to take me to the dance?"

"Yes. I do. Please don't say something sarcastic right now, Lo, because I can't handle it. I'm serious."

What is he thinking? Under any normal circumstances, I wouldn't be caught dead at a school dance. It's a nightmare in the flesh to me.

"I don't know what you want me to say."

"Say yes," he pleads. "Choose something good, something healthy. Live a little," he says. He cringes, realizing it is the wrong thing to say.

"I'm sorry, Cole. I can't," I say.

"You can. But you won't. You can never do anything for me. You're completely selfish, and you just use me for…I don't even know what." He slams his laptop lid shut, and I jump.

Who does he think he is?

"You know what?" I say, feeling a buried anger surfacing. "I'd rather eat glass than go to that stupid dance."

The look of hurt on Cole's face shocks me, but I'm committed now. And these feelings of anger are seductive. I've been numb for so long that even rage feels delicious. "I can't think of anything worse." I can't believe the words coming from my mouth.

"I'll ask someone else then," he says, firing back. "Maybe Sienna," he says. Sienna is a very gorgeous, very blond, very talented girl from our Media Arts class. She is the polar opposite of me.

"Fine," I say. "Ask her. What do I care?" It's a surprise, these feelings. I'm jealous when I imagine Sienna saying yes to his invitation. Why wouldn't she? I imagine how they will laugh and dance and feel joy together. All things I can't seem to do.

"I *will* ask her," he says. "At least Sienna is nice to me. Do you know how long it has been since someone said something nice to me? Sienna isn't the type of girl I go for, but maybe that's a good thing. So far my 'type' hasn't been good for me."

He stands up to leave but then sits back down in shock when he sees the tears running down my cheeks. I wipe them away.

"Snapshot, Lo," he says. "You're freaking me out."

"No, you don't get to do that," I say.

"Yes, I do," he says. "*Snapshot*, Logan. You tell me what's going on here, what's going on with us. What do you see? I'll tell you my snapshot. I see my beloved friend wasting her life because she's afraid."

I can't speak. That tidal wave of emotions is about to make landfall. Cole continues to talk, and all I can do is listen in pain.

"Sometimes I think if we didn't live so close to each other we wouldn't be friends," he says. "I know it has been hard. My mom didn't die, but did you know that my parents are probably splitting up?"

I look up at him. I had no idea.

"They're broke and fighting all the time. I didn't say anything to you because I thought you couldn't handle it. You have so much going on. But I thought with this stupid Broken Hearts Club, we could find a way to get it to help you too. Maybe you would start to see things for the way they are again."

"See what?" I manage.

"I'm in love with you, Lo," he says. "You know that."

"Maybe," I say. "But it doesn't matter. It's all doomed."

"What do you mean?" Cole asks. He is frustrated. "It doesn't have to be like that. You're grieving. Depressed. I think you need some help."

"That's not it. That's not the problem!" I shout at him.

"It is!" he shouts back.

"Stop it! Stop trying to make me love you!" I'm aware of footsteps on the stairs as we yell at each other.

"Why, Logan? *Why*?" Cole pleads with me.

"Because I'm going to die." The words come out as a wail, distorted from the lump in my throat and the tears that flow now. "I'm going to die and you'll have to watch and you'll never be the same again."

There is a brief silence, and a soft voice, Kelsey's, floats over the room.

"Time to go home now, Cole," she says. The kindness in her voice, coupled with the warmth of her hand on the back of my shoulder, is my undoing. I sob like I haven't in a year, not since the moment I woke up to a world without my mother.

Cole leaves.

Kelsey sinks onto the couch next to me. We stay like that for a long time before I realize that my dad is halfway down the stairs. I can see the tears on his cheeks.

Kelsey puts her arms around me, and I let her.

Chapter Six

If I thought being numb was difficult,
and that having my feelings on *mute*
was its own kind of purgatory, then I
had no idea what fresh hell it would
be to have my emotions come flooding
back all at once. Waking up the morning
after my fight with Cole is like waking
up with all my skin scrubbed off. Every
nerve and feeling seems brand new.

My mom always said that the truth is the key to freedom, and what I said to Cole was the truth. It seems like it was the thing that allowed my feelings to unleash, even if that truth is ugly and even if it's a truth that none of us wants to acknowledge.

I might have Huntington's disease.

Here's a snapshot of what the disease is like. It attacks your brain, causes you to lose all control of how you move, how you feel and how you think, until there's nothing left of what made you *you*. Many of the symptoms are similar to those of so many other diseases. Mom was depressed, but maybe that was because she knew she had the disease. She was irritable, but wouldn't you be? She couldn't control all these sudden jerky movements that came out of nowhere, and that made her self-conscious.

One time I heard Mom talking to Dad about it. She said the worst thing was not being able to learn new stuff anymore, and that her decision making was getting so bad that she couldn't even be responsible for her own child.

It wasn't long before Mom couldn't walk. Speaking took great effort. At the very end she couldn't swallow, and she was so thin I could lift her in my arms.

If I have Huntington's, I could make it to forty before all this happens to me. Is that long enough to live a life? It's more than some people get. Or I could get an early-onset form of the disease. I do have some mental issues, hello. But I'm not clumsy, and I'm not slurring my speech, so I'll take that as a good sign. My school performance, not so much. If I do have the juvenile version, I'm looking at ten decent years, tops. Oh, and here's a delightful tidbit. Because my mom had it, if I have it too, then something horrible called "anticipation" can occur, which means the disease appears even earlier.

The only way to know if I have it is to take a genetic test. So take it, right? Well, if I take it, and I find out I have it, then whatever future I have left will appear through the lens of terminal disease. A life of pain and decline. Sounds delightful, right?

Or I can live my life not knowing my status, keeping hope alive. But then I'll be afraid whenever I experience something that could be mistaken for a symptom. For example, something called blunted affect is an early sign of Huntington's. What's blunted affect? It means your emotions are not registering. Yeah.

At least I can take my feelings roaring back as a good sign. But man, I'd forgotten how much this hurts. I don't know if this is progress or what, but Dad and Kelsey say I'm on the right path. So far they've both just let me be this crying, leaking mess.

Dad keeps leaving tissues and cups of tea around, and he's hovering. But he's also avoiding talking about Huntington's. He doesn't want to deal with it at all.

As for Kelsey, well, she's around too. I'm not sure I noticed it happening, but she's always here. She doesn't live here—Dad would ask me about that first—but she might as well be. If someone had told me several months ago that Dad would have a new girlfriend, I would have told them they were high.

One thing Dad has not given me a break on is school. But there's no Cole showing up bright and early to drag me there. It's just my sorry self and my own feet getting me there. Not being with Cole is weird, but it's a relief. I can't be what he wants me to be right now.

Walking to school is kind of nice. It feels like an eternity since I looked at my neighborhood. The spring air is fresh, and everything is coming alive—birds, trees, the well-tended gardens of my neighbors. Today as I walk down our street, I notice that each home has its own little maple tree at the end of the drive. Some are taller than others and budding with fresh growth. Others are stunted and still bare. I pull out my Pentax and snap some shots of the dark brown branches against the bright, light-blue sky. But I know the black-and-white exposures will look like dark shots of lightning against a blown-out background. For the first time in a long while, I consider switching back to color film.

When I get to the end of my street and turn the corner onto the one that leads to my school, I notice the other students walking, the cars zooming by on their way to work. There's a whole world I've been blind to for months. It's like I had put on an emotional blindfold after Mom died. And the fight with Cole ripped it clean off.

With my camera in my hands and so many potential subjects all around me, I can't help but snap shots. I take sharp-focus, high-speed shots of people walking. I play with the depth of field so that the background is blurry and the people are in heightened detail.

I take close-ups of flowers peeking through cracks in the sidewalk. I manage to take a pretty detailed shot of a large black beetle stuck on a wad of gum.

"I know how you feel, little buddy," I say before nudging it to safety.

I hear the loud rumble of a motorcycle coming up the street, and I change my shutter speed to *bulb*—that's the setting that opens the shutter for as long as you have your finger on the trigger. It can let in a ton of light or a little, and the effect can be ghostly or blurry. In this case, once the motorbike comes into view, I press the shutter button and then pan the camera to focus on the bike as it rides by, releasing the button as it goes. If all works out, the shot will look as though the motorcycle is traveling at a hyper-fast speed, with trailing tracers of light and shadow coming from it. Now I really wish I had color film in my camera—the red taillight on the bike would have made such a cool effect. I vow to look for a roll of color film in my locker as soon as I get inside.

As I step onto the school grounds, I see the other students milling around, meeting friends, carrying their giant backpacks full of homework, sporting team jerseys and other uniforms and looking like real people. How did I not notice them before?

I'm acutely aware of Cole's car too. His dented white Toyota, unmistakable with its rust spots and single blue passenger door (the result of the donut fiasco), sits in the staff parking lot. He got here early today. Is he driving someone else around now? I put the idea out of my head. He has the right to do that if he wants. Still, I find myself eyeing his car as I walk past, trying to see if he's in there with someone. He's not. It's empty.

He's not leaning against my locker door when I get there either. I open it, gazing around the hall at the throng of students hurrying to first class. There's no sign of him, but his locker is on the other side of school from mine. I shuffle through the mess of my locker, past all the empty film canisters and scraps of paper, and grab my art notebook. Today I might have something to show Ms. Mill.

I notice my backup camera bag on the top shelf. Maybe there's some color film in there. I grab it and take it with me, slamming my locker door behind me. My arms are full, and I hurry down the hall to class.

I walk in before the bell and take my usual spot at the large table in the back. I dump my folder and camera bag on the table with a thump. Several people look up, but Cole, sitting near the front today, doesn't turn my way. Okay.

Ms. Mill walks in with her giant travel mug of coffee and overflowing briefcase and waves hello. "Workshop," she says, and I sigh in relief. She's giving us some free time in class to work on our projects. Was her weekend rough too?

I take the opportunity to search for a roll of color film in the camera case. I unzip it. My backup camera is a manual Leica, an old one. It's the camera I learned how to shoot with. Mom found it for me at an estate sale, and the owner didn't know how desirable these old Leicas are to true photographers. It needed work—it was missing a lens, and the inside seals were crumbling. But we fixed it up, and it has served me well, even if the shutter gets a little sticky at times.

I lift the compartment flap where I keep my film and see two empty canisters and one roll of color film. Success!

I pull out the camera to load it and notice that it still has Mom's Aztec-print camera strap attached to it. I had forgotten about it. How could I forget something like that?

"Hey," says someone with a sweet-sounding voice. "Cool camera. Leica, right?"

I look up and see that Sienna is talking to me from across the room, her golden hair cascading over the back of her chair. Cole glances over with a guilty look.

"Um, yeah," I say. *Great. She's pretty* and *she knows about cameras*.

"Can I see?" she asks.

"Sure," I say and watch as she approaches.

Cole, ever nosy, can't resist and comes over too. He leans against my table and gives me a quick smile.

I hand Sienna the camera, and she looks through the viewfinder. "I love these," she says. "My dad is into photography. I am too."

"Yeah?" I ask. "I thought you were more into podcasts and web series."

She nods. "But this is my first love." She hands the camera back. "Hey," she says, "we're going to the dance tomorrow night. That's cool, right?"

I swallow hard. This is awkward. "Yeah," I manage. "It's cool."

"Cool," says Sienna, smiling at Cole.

He changes the subject. "Hey, I haven't seen that one in a while." He points at the camera.

"Yeah, I'm going to put in some different film," I say. "Try something new." I turn the camera over and go to press the film-release button.

"Careful," Sienna says. "There's already a roll in there."

I check the camera back, and sure enough, there is already a half-used roll of color film in place.

"Whoa, how old is that?" Cole asks.

His eyes meet mine as we both realize something. The last time I used this camera was before my mom died. We had all gone down by the river and spent the day taking photos. That was the last day Mom left the house. Later that night she got into bed and never got out again.

I feel like all the air has been sucked from the room.

"Lolo?" Cole's voice comes to me as if underwater. "Lo, it's okay. It's all right."

"Cole," I say, finding my voice. "What is the date today?"

But he doesn't have to answer. I know.

In a few days it will be the one-year anniversary of my mother's death. And a few days after that it will be my eighteenth birthday.

"Death plus birthdays," I say, looking up at Cole.

He doesn't laugh though. Not this time.

Chapter Seven

I make it through the rest of the day in a haze, all my attention focused on the camera case I keep in my lap for every class. What's on there? What will I see? A happy family right before their world got ripped apart? No, that's what my mind is trying to trick me into seeing. We weren't happy, not for a long time. We were clutching each other, desperate to pretend that things would be okay. That we would be okay.

Cole follows me around for a little while until I tell him to leave me alone. I'm not mad anymore, but I need to deal with this by myself. He wants to come over after school while I develop the film, but this feels too private. I promise to text him later.

The world on my walk home is a lot less inspiring than it was this morning. I don't feel like taking any shots. All I can see are the few feet of gray sidewalk in front of me as I hurry back to my house.

When I get home, Dad is still at work, but Kelsey's SUV is in the driveway. I walk into the house through the side kitchen door and see her working on her laptop at our table. I forgot that there is a Broken Hearts Club meeting tonight. She looks up and smiles, then sees my face. Her smile disappears.

"Logan? You okay?" she asks.

I've gone mute, opening my mouth to say something, anything, but no sound comes.

Kelsey stands as if to come toward me with a hug, but I sidestep her and hurry past to the stairwell that leads to the basement. I can't talk right now. I can't think. I have to develop this film.

I get to the basement, dump my backpack and my jacket on the floor, unzip my camera case and remove my old Leica. I'll have to use up the last exposures on the roll before winding the film back into the canister, so I take eleven rapid photos of my feet framed against the orange-brown shag of the basement carpet.

I hesitate a moment after pressing the release button on the bottom of the camera. I have to turn the crank now to wind the film back in, but it has been sitting in the camera for a year. It could be brittle or stretchy, or it could snap off and fail to roll all the way back in.

I take a deep breath and turn the crank. I feel some resistance and turn a little harder, and then it starts to give and cranks until I feel the spool spinning, unattached.

I'm not going to pull up on the crank to release the camera's back flap until I'm safe in darkness. I don't want to risk exposing any of the film to light. Cradling my camera in my arms, I pull back the first door to my darkroom, step through and then shut it behind me. I switch off the light and step through the second door. I secure that behind me, too, and flip the little lever lock I installed on the inside. It feels safer this way, for my film and for me.

At last, I am in darkness. I would use a red safelight for the first stages of development with my black-and-white film and papers, but color film is different, so I'm going to keep it dark. That's fine, because I could do this in my sleep. I keep all my supplies in the same order in the same spot.

I pull open the back of my camera and take out the film canister, then pull part of the film out and slip it into my developing reel, careful not to touch or scratch the surface of the film. I wind it on, then place that reel into my development canister and pour in my developer fluid. I agitate, press the button on my trusty kitchen timer, and then pour it out into the basin. Next I add the fixer, press the timer again and wait, listening to the seconds tick by. Then I pour that out and rinse well with water from a jug. Once it's all rinsed, I clip the end of the film onto my line and let it hang while I pour over the wetting agent to prevent water spots as the film dries. The liquid drips into an old laundry tub my dad scored for me.

At this point I turn on my dim safe-light. The film is fixed, so it won't develop further, but I'm not taking any chances. Now I need to let it dry for two hours before cutting it into strips to make the prints.

As I exit the darkroom, my phone buzzes inside my backpack. I never bring it into the darkroom with me—it's too distracting, and if it glowed, it could ruin my film.

I fish it out and look at the screen. It's Cole.

C: HEY
L: hey
C: ...
L: ?
C: WHAT'S IN THE BOX?

Of course Cole had to insert a *Se7en* movie reference right now. I text back.

L: You did not just Brad Pitt me.
C: I could not help it.
L: You've been waiting ALL DAY to do that.
C: I have. You know me so well.

I'm smiling in spite of myself.

L: I developed it. Drying now. Waiting.
C: Didn't peek?
L: Couldn't. Want to make prints first.
C: Can I come see?

I hesitate.

L: Not tonight, k?
C: k...say hi to everyone at the meeting. And tell Humphrey I have something for him. I will call him tomorrow.
L: What? Is it Zelda?
C: Hey, I've got secrets too. L8R...

Great, he's holding out on me now. What does he have for Humphrey? I'd better get a move on with tonight's snacks and setup. Everyone will be here soon.

I go up to the kitchen and see that Kelsey is already cutting fruit and cheese for a tasting board, arranging the slices of cheese with bunches of grapes. She places a scattering of mixed olives on another board with some draped cold cuts and crusty bread. It looks delicious, and I sneak an olive. She sees me out of the corner of her eye and smiles.

"How was your day?" she asks as she hands me the trays to take downstairs.

"Weird," I say.

She smiles again. "So many of my days are weird."

"Really?" I ask. Kelsey seems like the kind of woman who always has it together. "You?"

She looks stunned. "Yes, me. A couple of years ago I was married to my high school sweetheart, we were trying to have kids, and a routine test revealed his cancer. He was gone within months." She stops talking and hovers at the top of the stairs.

"I'm sorry," she says. "That just sort of bubbled out."

"No," I say. "It's fine. It's good, I think."

We walk down the stairs to the basement, and Kelsey offers me some of the cheese. We both sit on the couch and dig in, guests be damned.

"It was intense," she says, chewing on a piece of bread. "Everything I knew and understood about the world was wrong. Up was down, you know?"

I nod. I know what she means. "So," I ask, not sure if I'm pushing it, "how did you...move on?"

Kelsey raises her eyebrows. "Move on? You mean to your dad?"

"Yeah."

She offers me some grapes, and I pick them off. I haven't been this hungry in a long time.

"I guess I didn't move on," she says. "The truth is, if my husband, Ben, came back today, I'd be with him in an instant. And I suspect it's the same for your dad."

Of course she's right.

"But," she says, "that doesn't mean we have to stop caring for and loving people while we're alive. I can't think of a better tribute to my husband than to continue on in life with an open heart."

I know what she's saying is right. "But," I ask, "*how* do you do it?"

Kelsey reaches over and takes my hand. I get a flash of my mother in my mind.

"You try. Try every day, and it gets a tiny bit easier."

Overhead we hear Dad's heavy footfalls.

"Is it me, or does he walk like a rhino?" Kelsey asks, and we both laugh.

Tonight's Broken Hearts Club meeting turns into more of a surprise party for me. I guess they all, *somehow*, found out it's my birthday soon. Everyone wants to give me a present now, because our next meeting isn't for a couple of weeks.

The first gift I get is from Dad and Kelsey, who chipped in to get me a stack of high-quality photo paper and a neutral-density filter for my camera. The filter keeps too much daylight from entering the camera. I can use it with a slow shutter speed when I'm taking shots of the river.

One of the lawyers gives me a fancy pen set. (I think it was Jim. Or maybe it was Other Jim?) Grace gives me a custom T-shirt with a photo of me holding a camera up as I take a photo. It's meta in the best way, and I love it so much that I have the urge to hug her.

"Go ahead, child," she says. "I don't bite."

I lean in and put my arms around her. It's like sinking into a pile of warm dough covered in a wooly sweater. It's the best.

Humphrey saves his gift for last, handing me a heavy gift bag with hearts all over it.

"You shouldn't have," I say as I take it from him.

"Yes, I should," he says and watches as I lift the tissue paper and pull out the gift. It's a lamp, but not any old lamp. It's a neon tube lamp bent into the shape of a lopsided heart. I rush to plug it in, and when I do its light is blinding. It's the greatest thing ever.

"Whoa," says Dad. "Turn that thing down. I'm sure they can see it from space!"

I click it off and am left with an impression of the neon heart burned into my retinas, so that everywhere I look around the room, the heart shape is superimposed. There's Grace with a heart next to her. Lawyers Jim, Jim and John with hearts. Dad and Kelsey, also with hearts. Humphrey, sweet Humphrey, with a blazing heart dead center in his chest.

I have the best idea. And not a jump-from-the-roof idea—a save-my-Media-Arts-project idea.

I throw my arms around Humphrey. He is the exact opposite of Grace. He's all bones, but still warm. "Thank you, Humphrey," I say.

"Of course, lovey," he says.

"Oh, that reminds me. Cole says he has something for you," I say.

"For me?" asks Humphrey.

I shrug. "He said he would call you tomorrow."

"Okay then," he says. "Now, if you would do me a favor, lovey?"

"Anything."

"Switch that gorgeous lamp back on."

I grin. "You got it."

I switch it on and it beams to life. All anyone can do is stare.

Later, after everyone is gone, I head to my darkroom to make some prints and work on my Media Arts project. Humphrey's gift has inspired an idea, a way of "drawing" over images with light, but in a more organic way than using Photoshop or something. I'm going to use my photos of the Broken Hearts Club members.

I'm going to blow the prints up large, cut out shapes in the prints and then mount the final photos onto light boxes so the light beams through. I'm thinking of doing an image of Humphrey with a heart in his chest, and maybe the shape of a person standing next to Grace. It will be a way to add what they're missing. And each of us has something missing.

I take down the clip of old film I had drying and examine the exposures. A lot of them are grainy because the film was breaking down. I'm disappointed to see that most of the shots are scenery shots. Not a single one has Mom in it. There is one exposure I decide to print. It's a self-timer photo I took of myself by the river. In my memory I can see Mom off frame, so I'm going to develop this one and "draw" her in.

I get to work, knowing I will be in here all night until I get it right.

Chapter Eight

It's the day of the dance. It's also a year to the day since my mom died. Death plus dancing. But I won't be dancing. I'll leave that to Cole and Sienna.

When I wake, I look out my bedroom window and see that the sky is clear and blue. That's annoying. This is definitely a rain kind of day.

After I get dressed in my usual uniform of black jeans and black top, I look in my closet at the sea of black and fish out a bright blue scarf my mom gave me. It's a long wrap, made of some kind of fancy material that is so soft it brings tears to my eyes. Mom bought it on a trip to Paris when she was a little older than me. I've never worn it. I've always been afraid that it would get lost or ruined, but that's stupid. Here is this gorgeous thing sitting in my closet. If I died tomorrow, I would never have enjoyed it.

I smell the scarf, feeling its softness on my face, and then drape it around me. I look in the mirror. It's like covering myself in a piece of sky. I vow to wear this scarf every single day from now on.

When I walk into the kitchen, I kind of expect to see Kelsey, but she's not here. Dad says nothing as he buzzes around and gets coffee and toast going for us, but I understand. Today is not a day for new girlfriends. It's not a day for anyone.

Dad hands me toast with jam, and I cram it into my mouth. He gives me a cautious look.

"Okay?" he asks.

"Yes, Father, your toast skills are adequate," I say.

He rolls his eyes and mutters something about teenagers.

"But yes," I add. "I'm okay. In fact, over the last few days I have made a lot of progress on my project."

"Really?" He whirls around from the counter, butter knife in hand. "Can I see?" he asks.

"Nope," I say, taking my coffee to go. "It's a surprise. You'll see it at the end-of-term art show."

"You're...you're going to...participate?" he asks. He's almost trembling with excitement.

I laugh and start to leave him with his toast. But I think better of it and turn back to give him a sudden hug.

"Oh," he says. "Thank you."

I'm getting better at this hugging thing.

"Do you need me today, Dad?" I ask.

He looks at me and touches the scarf, caressing it between his fingers. He shakes his head. "No, I need you to go to school. And I need to go to work."

"Okay, I'll see you later?" I ask.

He swallows. "I will be here. I'll grab some Chinese takeout on the way home."

"Maybe we could watch a movie," I suggest.

"Sure. A comedy," he says.

"So nothing about dead wives or moms then?"

He shakes his head. "I was asking for that, wasn't I?"

"Sorry."

"Get your butt to school!" He gives me a little push as he places another piece of toast in my hand.

I grab my backpack and head out the door. As it shuts behind me, I look back at my dad. He has a smile on his face. He's going to be okay.

I'm a little behind schedule, but what else is new? I have to hurry to get to school so I can talk to Ms. Mill before class. I'm kind of half walking, half jogging when I hear the familiar high-pitched squeal of Cole's Toyota pulling up alongside me.

"Hey!" he calls out. "Want a ride? Hop in."

I can't be late, so I open the door and get in, avoiding eye contact. It's still so awkward between us.

"Hey," I manage.

"Hey," he says. "I wasn't sure you'd be here today."

I shrug. "Life goes on and all that crap."

"Yeah," he says.

We drive in silence the rest of the way to school. When we pull into the teachers' lot, I hop out before he can cut the ignition. I offer a quick "thanks" and speed walk toward the school.

"Lo!" he calls after me.

I turn around as he hurries out of the car. He's in such a rush that he doesn't bother to shut the door behind him.

"What?" I ask.

He jams his hands into his pockets, looking nervous. "Tonight's the dance, remember?"

I nod. *Not this again.*

"I wanted to make sure it's okay that I'm going with Sienna," he says.

"Cole, you're free to do whatever you want."

"I know, but—"

"Please don't ask me again," I say.

He nods. "Okay." He walks back to his car.

I go inside and make my way to Ms. Mill's office, a tiny room attached to the Media Arts lab.

Ms. Mill is already there, drinking coffee from her enormous travel mug and surrounded by piles of papers and folders on her desk. I don't know if I've ever looked around her office before, but the walls are covered in film posters, concert bills and artifacts of what looks like a wild youth.

I knock. She doesn't look up. She waves me in and motions to the seat in front of her. I sit.

"Hang on a sec," she says as she scribbles something on a huge notepad.

"I've got to get this idea down before it leaves my head." She puts down her pen. "There. Hello."

"Hi," I say. "Working on a project?"

"Yes, a screenplay."

"Wow, that's cool," I say.

"And you? Have you been working on *your* project?" she asks.

For once I'm not filled with anxiety over this question.

"I have," I say, pulling out a folder from my backpack. I select the enlarged image of Humphrey and hold it up to the desk lamp. The illuminated cutout heart glows in his center.

Ms. Mill gives a low whistle.

I pull out another image, this one of Grace with the cutout shape of her son standing next to her. I hold it up to the light, and Ms. Mill nods.

"I see what you're going for," she says. "What are you going to use, light boxes?"

"Yes, but I'm going to need a bunch of them. And I only have two. Any chance I could use some from the lab?"

Ms. Mill thinks for a moment. "I have a better idea," she says. "How about one really big light box?"

She fills me in on her idea to swipe the light-up portable scoreboard from the boys' basketball team. I decide then that Ms. Mill is my hero. We spend the last few minutes before class plotting and talking about my project, and by the time we're done, I feel like I can face the rest of this day.

I avoid talking to Cole and Sienna during class. There is too much energy between us all, what with Sienna talking to her friends about her dress and blah, blah, blah. I spend the whole class working on my project and planning more photo cutouts. The dimensions of the large lighted board will allow me to create a collage of six large portraits, so I have more work to do. The rest of my classes go by fast because I'm daydreaming so much. Since the whole school is dance obsessed, none of my teachers bother me.

I hurry home, avoiding the front of the school where Cole could be waiting to offer me a ride. I head straight to my darkroom, where I work on my project until I'm surprised by a knock on the door. It's Dad, back already.

"Honey? I've got the Chinese food. Come get it while the grease is still... greasy."

"Be right there," I call and finish clipping up the last of my prints.

Dad spreads out the food on our coffee table, and we both sit cross-legged and dig in, not bothering with plates. We pass the containers back and forth as we watch Dad's all-time favorite movie, *Monty Python and the Holy Grail*. Dad laughs so hard I'm afraid he's going to choke on his chow mein.

By the end of the film, we're both so full we can't move. I catch Dad trying to subtly check his phone.

"Dad," I say.

"Hmm?" He turns to me.

"Call Kelsey." I know he wants to.

"No, this is our day," he says.

"Parents," I say, shaking my head. "This isn't 'our day'—this is 'a' day. A shitty day, but still only a day."

"Language," he says, but he's smiling.

"Sorry. You know what I mean."

"I know," he says.

"We can't be chaining ourselves to these sad rituals," I say. "Even if the food is good." I grab another egg roll and see if I can manage another bite, but no, I'm cashed out.

Dad stares at me. "When did you get so wise? And so hungry?"

I shrug. "I don't know. I guess I'm smarter than you."

"Teenagers. Okay, if you're sure. I do want to call Kelsey."

"Good," I say, struggling to stand up. "I'm going to take a walk, digest some of this food and take some more photos for my project."

"Not too long," he says. "And be safe."

I give him a high five, grab my camera and head up the stairs.

Once I'm outside, the fresh evening air gives me a boost. I snap photos as I walk. These aren't for my project, but I need something to do.

I end up walking past the school, and the dance is in full swing. I can hear the faint *whoomp* of electronic bass coming through the gymnasium walls. Cole's car is in the lot.

Don't do it, Logan. Don't you dare go in that school. But I can't help it. I want a peek.

I go in through a side door and take the hallway to the gym's stage access. From there I can watch from the wings without anyone seeing me. As I walk past props from hundreds of past school productions, I hear the music change from a fast-paced hip-hop track to a slow dance. Great, right on time for the cheese.

I peek out from behind the stage curtain. There are a lot of people here, many more than I expected. I thought school dances attracted smallish groups of sentimental dance freaks, but it turns out that, nope, it's a normal thing to do.

Everyone is coupled up, with a few stragglers standing along the sidelines looking as uncomfortable as I would be. I'm safe from my vantage point, so I take shots of the couples. As I scan the room, my lens finds Cole and Sienna, slow dancing, arms around each other, looking like the perfect couple I knew they would make.

Snapshot, Logan. My mom in my mind again. Okay, Mom, snapshot. I feel like a wildlife photographer studying normal teenagers in their habitat. I feel like a perpetual outsider. I feel like it should be me, or some better version of me, dancing with Cole.

As I watch them sway, I am filled with regret for everything I'm missing out on. I know Mom would have wanted me to live.

I slip out of the gym unnoticed. As I make my way back home through the darkened streets, I know what I have to do. It's almost my birthday. And it's impossible to move forward when you're not sure if your days are numbered.

I have to end this fear once and for all.

Chapter Nine

A few days later, I wake up with a lead weight in my stomach. It's my birthday, and I have to break my dad's heart.

I get dressed, knowing he's going to be waiting in the kitchen to take me to the diner for pancakes, as he's done every year of my life. Can I do this?

I go to the kitchen, and sure enough Dad is there. So is Kelsey, and the two of them bust out singing as soon as they see me.

"*Happy birthday, dear Logan...*"

I let them finish, struggling to smile.

"So, honey, how does it feel to be a year older?" Dad beams at me.

Kelsey takes a few pics of me with her phone.

"It's underwhelming," I say.

"Teenagers," Dad says to Kelsey, his smile huge.

I'm not looking forward to this.

"Ready for breakfast?" Kelsey asks.

I clear my throat. "I need my dad to come somewhere with me."

Dad's eyebrows push together a little, and I can tell he's getting worried.

"Sure," says Kelsey. "I'll see you guys later."

Dad shrugs, and we go out to the car.

I ask him to drive us to the bench, Mom's bench, and he does.

We sit and look at the river swirling past, the trees bending over the water and the birds flitting overhead.

Dad turns to me, waiting. He breaks the ice. "You're not pregnant, are you?"

"What? God, Dad, no!"

He lets out a huge breath. "Thank God. That was tense. But for the record, I do want to be a grandpa one day. Just not yet!" He chuckles and then stops when he sees the look on my face.

"Honey, what is it?" he asks.

"That's the thing, Dad. I don't know if I can have kids," I tell him.

"What—?" he starts, but I interrupt.

"Please let me say this."

He nods. "Go ahead."

"It's not that Mom died. I mean, that's not the only thing that has been making it so hard for me lately. It's that I don't know if I have a future," I say.

He opens his mouth to say something but doesn't.

I continue, "I don't know if I can fall in love or get married or have kids. I don't know if I will see the world or have a career or grow old." I'm crying now, and because Dad gets it, he's crying too.

"I can't live like this anymore, not knowing if I have Huntington's," I say.

Dad reaches out and takes my hand.

"I can't have this hanging over me forever." I take a deep breath. "So I scheduled a genetic test. It's today, and I need you to come with me."

Dad's face crumples for a moment, but he pulls it together.

"But," he starts, his voice hoarse, "it's your birthday. Pancakes."

"I know," I say. "Pancakes."

We sit in silence, staring at each other, and then Dad takes my other hand.

"Logan, if this is what you need to do, then let's go do it."

"You understand?" I ask.

"I do," he says. "And I've been waiting for this day. I thought maybe I had more time, that you needed to get a little older. But you've grown so much this year. And I'm so proud of you."

"Thanks, Dad."

We take a last look at the river, and then I go to meet my destiny.

Snapshot, Logan. Who are you at eighteen? Here is a birthday snapshot, Mom. Dad and I are waiting in the genetic counselor's office at the hospital. For some stupid reason I thought I would find out the results today, but it turns out it doesn't happen that quickly.

A brilliant and kind woman named Dr. Jensen takes my blood and talks to me about the risks. Dad and I listen, but she understands from our story that we know the risks all too well. She does take a moment to explain what they're looking for. She also makes a point to tell me that I can stop the process at any time if I'm not ready to find out.

There's a change in a certain gene that involves something called a "CAG repeat." People who have Huntington's, like my mom, have a higher number of CAG repeats than healthy people do. When you have a high number of CAG repeats, the gene stretches out and expands too much, and that causes the disease. That's the simple version, anyway. The actual science is so complicated it makes my head spin.

My blood sample contains my DNA, and it will be sent to the lab to be analyzed. Some smart people will use their special machines to count how many CAG repeats I have. If I have fewer than twenty-seven, then I'm negative for Huntington's, and I can live my life free of the disease, and everything will be rainbows and unicorns. Plus, my future kids will be fine too.

If I have, like, more than forty CAG repeats, I'm screwed.

There is a gray area between the two extremes, and I'm hoping not to get caught there either. I've been living in a gray area for such a long time. I need a definitive answer.

As I sit through Dr. Jensen's talk, I wonder if this is what Mom went through when she was diagnosed. It sounds weird, but it makes me feel closer to her.

The appointment doesn't take long. The doctor sends us off with a warm smile that I'm sure she must have practiced in the mirror. I don't know how she does this every day.

The drive back home is quiet until Dad gets the nerve to speak. "You hungry?" he asks.

I look at him and grin.

"Pancakes," we say in unison.

It's a little over half an hour since I took a life-altering test. My dad and I are in the diner, stuffing ourselves with pancakes topped with vanilla ice cream. I shove the last of my stack into my mouth and lean back in the booth.

Dad wipes his mouth with a napkin. "So," he says, "what's next for today?"

"Don't you have to go in to work?" I ask.

He shakes his head. "Nah, it's not a big deal."

"Well, I should try to get to school."

"Honey, school's over in a few minutes."

"Yeah, I know, but we're having an

extra students-only Media Arts lab after school to get ready for the final show. Like a peer review. I should go."

"Okay," he says. "I'll drop you off on the way. One thing though."

"What?" I ask.

"Can you help me out of this booth?" He groans. "I ate enough pancakes to choke an elephant."

I laugh and take his hand.

Chapter Ten

Dad drops me off at school. I'm only about fifteen minutes late for the Media Arts lab. Ms. Mill has been pretty hands off these last couple weeks. She's trying to get us to take responsibility for our own destinies. It's the theme of my life these days.

I hurry down the hall, and as I approach the Media Arts room, I hear a familiar voice echoing through the door. It takes me a moment to place the voice. It's relaying things so personal it takes my mind a moment to understand what's happening.

The voice is my voice.

The door is open a few inches. I peek inside.

The lights are off, and a few of the students are seated in a semicircle in front of a screen. There's rough movie footage playing, and I'm in it. This must be Cole's final project. But it's not finished. There are long pauses and no transitions and random footage in between. He must be nervous about it. I can see him chewing his thumbnail, casting glances at the viewers' faces.

There are other people in the film too—members of the Broken Hearts Club. Humphrey talking about baby Zelda. Then a scene shot from afar in a mall food court. Humphrey approaches a woman in her sixties, and they embrace. Zelda! It must be. For a moment I am filled with happiness, but it is short lived. I am back on the screen.

Except it's not the current me. It's me from almost a year ago, from right after Mom died. I'm crying and telling Cole something that I don't remember him filming. In the video, we're in his room, and the camera angle is weird. I'm barely in frame.

As I watch the video, I glance at Cole, who looks uncomfortable. He is frowning at the screen like he doesn't recognize his own work. He *should* be uncomfortable. What I'm seeing is evidence of the worst thing he has ever done. The single most heinous of all his oh-so-wonderful ideas.

I stare at my crying face, blown up large on the screen. Each word I say is like a punch straight to the heart.

"*…she was my best friend. She used to call me her little wolf, and I used to snuggle with her in bed when she was too sick to get out.*"

The next words cause me to fling open the door of the Media Arts room and stride in. I am glowing with anger.

"*…I fell asleep, and when I woke up she was cold. I didn't know she was dead. I missed it, her last moments. I understood when I touched her. And that coldness has never gone away. It got inside of me and it will never go away…*"

Cole sees me at the last moment, and I can see tears in his eyes.

"IS IT A GOOD SHOW?" I scream.

I open the projector and rip out the DVD.

Cole has enough sense to not even look at me, but I want him to see this.

"Look at me!" I demand, and he lifts his eyes to meet mine. On his face is shame and regret so deep that I have to look away.

"How *could* you?" I snap the DVD in half. "Now you know what it's like to lose something."

I toss the broken disc to the floor and run out of the room.

This is too much. My birthday, the test, my uncertain future and now this. My best friend using the most painful moment of my life for a movie. I feel so sick that I vomit pancakes into the hallway trash can.

Snapshot, Cole. How does it feel to know that we are through?

Chapter Eleven

Betrayal is a special kind of poison. You think it will kill you in the moment, but then it keeps killing you over and over again every time you think about it. For days I wallow in my darkroom, avoiding the constant texts from Cole:

C: Can we talk? I'm so sorry.
C: Please let me explain.

C: Please call me.

The upside is I've almost finished my project. I have one final image left to mount. It's a photo of Cole sitting by himself on the curb, looking lonely and beautiful. At first I wanted to destroy it, but I can't. As angry and hurt as I am, when I look at his photo I feel the years of love between us. I set it aside. There's time.

Time is all I've got right now. Waiting for the results of my genetic test has been pure torture. I don't know how Dad is getting through it. He's been humming around here like a busy and cheerful little bee. Maybe he thinks he can't fall apart. Or maybe he's saving it for when we get the bad news.

We're supposed to go back to the hospital tomorrow to find out. I can't shake the feeling that it's going to be the worst outcome.

Despite all this, we're having a Broken Hearts Club meeting tonight. Dad has not let me off the hook. I am still responsible for refreshments. Genetic death sentence plus fruit tray, I think as I trudge upstairs to make snacks.

Kelsey is here already, and I walk in on them kissing. It's not a little smooch, but a full-on make-out session. It's disgusting and sweet at the same time.

"Ew, you guys," I say, announcing my presence.

"OH!" Dad says, way too loud. "You came out of hiding."

"Yeah," I say as I open the fridge.

"Let me give you a hand," Kelsey says.

Dad disappears to tidy the basement, and she and I set to work preparing the food.

"So what's up with you and Cole?" Kelsey asks.

I sigh and put down the paring knife. "He filmed me talking about my mom. About being with her when she died. And he included it in his film project."

She winces. "Oh, Cole."

"Yeah. He's a bonehead that way. He doesn't think sometimes."

Kelsey is quiet for a moment, and then she says, "Well, he cares about you so much. I don't think he'd ever deliberately do anything to hurt you, would he?"

I pick up the knife again and chop, taking my anger out on carrots and celery. "No, you know what? I don't think he did it on purpose either. But it's typical Cole selfish bullshit. And it's annoying and dumb. He's annoying and dumb!"

I'm chopping with vigor now, ranting at Kelsey, who is patiently listening. "I hate that he makes me feel this way, that he has the power to make me feel this way. I wish I wasn't in love with him! Damn it!" The tip of the paring knife catches on a tough piece of carrot and slices into the tip of my pinky. The pain shoots through my finger. I'm dripping blood.

"Great," I say. "Now he made me cut myself."

Kelsey grabs a clean tea towel and wraps it around my hand. She holds it up over my head.

"You know," she says with a smile, "you're maybe being a little hard on him, considering you're in love with him."

I sigh, trying not to smile back. I fail. "Yeah, I know."

"Maybe," she says, unwrapping my finger to take a look, "you could give him another chance?"

My finger isn't that bad. It's just a little slice. Kelsey cleans it, applies ointment and puts a bandage on it. Having her do this for me brings tears to my eyes. I have to fight them off. To her credit, she acts like she doesn't notice.

"I'll take care of the snacks," she says. "Blood plus snacks isn't the greatest combo."

I give her a quick hug. I turn to go downstairs, but before I do, I say, "I'm glad my dad found you. That we found you."

Kelsey doesn't turn around. She stops chopping for a moment and says, "Me too."

Tonight's Broken Hearts Club meeting is packed, with all the regulars here and a bunch of newbies. Then Humphrey walks in with two more unexpected people. The first is the woman from Cole's footage—Zelda! The other is Cole.

"What. Are. You. Doing. Here," I say through clenched teeth.

Cole starts to say something, but Humphrey steps in. "Now, now, lovey," he says. "I wanted him to come so I could introduce my daughter, Zelda, to everyone." Humphrey says the words *my daughter* with such pride.

I turn to her and hold out my unbandaged hand. "Hi, Zelda, I'm Logan. It's great to meet you."

She ignores my hand and hugs me instead. "Logan, I'm so happy to meet you! You have no idea what you and Cole have done for me. I've wanted to know my father my whole life, and now he's here!"

I struggle to find words. "You're welcome," is all I manage.

Humphrey takes Zelda around the room. I'm left alone with Cole.

I scowl at him, but he looks so broken that I give it up. It's not a fair fight anymore.

"Lo," he says. "I won't stay. I wanted to see you for just a minute. To tell you that I'm so sorry. I didn't know that piece of footage was on there. I forgot that I had filmed it at all."

"Why did you film it?" I ask.

"I didn't mean to. You came over all of a sudden while I was working on my stop-animation film. You remember the one with the plasticine? And I forgot to turn the camera off. And then you were saying all this stuff. Later I realized it recorded you, but I didn't feel like I could delete it. I thought maybe I should save it for you. I don't know. I wish it had never happened."

It's coming back to me now. "Yeah," I say. "I remember that project. It was, like, little tiny clay people, right?"

"Right," he says. "It was a love story."

"Whatever happened in the end?" I ask.

He shrugs. "I don't know. I guess I gave up."

We stare at each other for what seems like forever. I know I can't stay angry with him. He didn't mean to hurt me, and the only reason he is even capable of that is because we're so close.

I change the subject. "So a lot of heavy stuff has happened."

He doesn't miss a beat. "Like what?" He grabs a bowl of cheesy chips and starts munching.

"I got the test," I say, and he stops eating. He knows what I mean.

For a second his face registers pure terror, and then he composes himself. "And did you find out…"

"Tomorrow," I say.

"Want me to come?" he asks.

I shake my head. "Only my dad."

"Of course," he says.

Someone turns up the music a little, and Cole reaches out to take my hand. I let him. He leads me to the darkroom and we slip inside, turning on the blue light.

He studies the photos I have clipped to the line. "Wow," he says. "Are these for your project?"

"Yep."

"It's amazing," he says, turning to me. "You're amazing."

I've missed him so much. Having him so close to me is making me feel things I haven't felt in a long time. The way he's looking at me turns my insides to jelly. Enough with fear. I grab him by the sweater and kiss him.

And this is it, the thing I've been dreaming about but denying myself.

A kiss from a boy I have loved for my entire life. It's the sweetest moment I've had in so long. And the warmest rush of love I've felt since I can remember. I feel alive.

When we pull away, Cole looks wobbly. "Whoa," he says, and then pulls it together enough to add, "Keanu-level whoa."

"You are such a huge dork," I say.

"But you love me?" he asks.

"Yes. I love you," I say. Relief floods through me.

He grins and leans into me. "So we're back together then?"

"Don't push it."

He laughs. "Kidding. I was thinking we can hang out, you know. Maybe watch some old flicks?"

"So, like, what we always do?" I ask.

"Yeah," he says, moving closer, placing a hand on the wall behind me. "But with more making out."

His shirt sleeve slides up his bicep. I swear it's all I can do not to reach out and touch his arm. So I do. Screw it.

His face falls toward mine.

"I'm sorry I destroyed your project," I whisper.

He smiles. "It's okay. I always have a backup. But I deleted all the footage of you. I put it on a separate disk for you, if you want it."

I nod. "Thanks."

His lips brush against mine again, and I swear I feel like I'm going to dissolve into nothing. There's a knock on the door. I hear Grace call my name.

Cole groans. "Great timing."

I slide open the door. "Hi, what is it?"

"Logan, honey, the phone is for you," she says.

"Oh, thanks." I walk out of the dark-room to pick up the receiver.

This is weird. No one ever calls me on the house phone.

"Hello?" I say.

"Logan, this is Dr. Jensen, from genetic counseling."

You know that thing in the movies when time stops for everyone but the main character? When all the people are frozen in mid-action and the star of the film turns around to view their entire world falling apart? Yeah, that's me, right now.

Chapter Twelve

It's a strange experience, holding the phone to my ear and listening to my heart pound in my chest. All around me the members of the Broken Hearts Club eat, socialize, laugh and move through time and space as if nothing is amiss. Dr. Jensen repeats my name.

"Logan? Logan? Are you there?" Her voice is as gentle as it was in her office.

I swallow hard, my throat as dry as sand. I grab a can of root beer from the sideboard, crack it and down it. I have the sudden irrational thought that this might be the last beverage I enjoy before I find out I'm dying.

"Yes," I croak. "I'm here."

Cole is at my side, but I turn away. I don't want him to see my face right now. Why is she calling? Why now? It must be really bad if she's calling at this time of night. I bet I have the highest number of CAG repeats in history. I bet they want to study me.

"Logan," Dr. Jensen says, "are you by yourself right now? Is your dad there?"

"I'm..." It's a struggle to form words, and I search the faces in the crowd around me. They all seem to blur into one another. Dad, where is Dad?

And then he's there, walking toward me with his worried face on.

"He's here," I say. "I'm not alone. Go ahead, Dr. Jensen. Tell me."

"Good, that's good. Listen, I wanted to spare you the visit tomorrow and give you some peace of mind. I never call people with bad news. I always do that in person."

The music stops, and it's not in my mind. Dad has turned it off and is staring at me. I look at Cole, and all the color has gone from his face.

Wait. What? "You mean…?"

"You have a perfectly normal number of CAG repeats, Logan," says Dr. Jensen. "Twenty-three of them. Ideal," she says. I can feel her smile through the phone.

"Twenty-three?" I ask, not believing it at first. "I don't have Huntington's?"

Dad looks like his knees are going to give out.

"No, Logan. As far as I am concerned, you're perfectly healthy. And I am so happy to be able to tell you that. You and your dad are welcome to still come see me tomorrow to pick up a copy of the results and have a chat if you wish. But I think perhaps you could use a break from all this, correct? I can have it forwarded to your family doctor."

I'm stunned. I manage a weak "thank you" and then pass the phone to Dad, who takes over and begins asking Dr. Jensen all the things I didn't think of. But the result is the same—I'm okay.

Dad hangs up the phone and grabs me, crushing me in a hug. "She's okay!" he shouts. Everyone starts to gather around us, patting me on the shoulder, hugging me, telling me how happy they are. Humphrey is crying with relief, and Grace kisses my cheek. Kelsey and Dad are clutching each other. It's all too much.

I turn to Cole, who gives me a bewildered shake of his head before holding me close. He takes my face in his hands and says, "From now on, can you not scare me like that? I think my heart actually stopped beating."

I can't help but grin. "If you think that's bad, get a load of this." Then I give him "the eyes."

"Not 'the eyes'!" he says, staggering backward to fall on the couch.

I flop down next to him and we rest there, staring up at the stained popcorn ceiling of my basement. That glorious, hideous, perfect ceiling that we've been staring at our whole lives.

"Cole?" I ask.

"Lolo?"

"Let's go places, okay? Let's go everywhere."

He turns to me. "I'll go anywhere with you, Lo. Paris, Antarctica, the moon, wherever."

"Good, because I need a ride," I say.

He laughs. "I love you."

"Ditto," I say.

He sighs. "Patrick Swayze in *Ghost* reference, check. Big adorable eyes, check. Not dying of a horrible disease, check. Yeah. Pretty much my dream girl."

I rest my head on his shoulder, and before I know it, despite the noise and bustle and energy in the room, I'm fast asleep.

I dream of a cave. It's cold, but I'm wrapped in warmth and love. It feels like Mom. It feels safe, and it has been so long since I felt safe.

When I wake up, it's late. The Broken Hearts Club is long gone, and so is Cole. Dad sits in the armchair, reading through a box of papers. They look like letters.

I sit up, rubbing the grit from my eyes. "Hey, Dad. Is Kelsey still here?" I ask.

He shakes his head. "I have something I want to give you," he says. He comes and sits next to me.

He hands me a handwritten note. I recognize the shaky scrawl of Mom's handwriting. I read it and then fold it up again. I'm filled with the wish that she could have been spared from her pain.

"Your mom always planned on making tons of these notes for you to read after she was gone, but it became hard for her to even stay awake, let alone talk or write. She tried. But she was also worried that if she left you constant reminders of her death, you'd never move on."

I nod. I understand.

He continues, "She always said the worst thing wasn't dying. The worst thing was leaving you. As a mom, her greatest wish was that you would live a happy life, even if it meant you had to forget her in order to do it."

"I could never forget her," I whisper. "Never." It's true. Mom is like a missing part of my body, like a limb or a vital organ. How do you forget your arm? How do you forget your own heart?

"I know," he says. "I can't either."

Dad kisses the top of my head. "I'm exhausted," he says. "But I'm here if you need me."

After Dad goes to bed, I take a photo of the note. I'm going to use it in my project as the center image. It's the perfect thing.

Chapter Thirteen

The next time the Broken Hearts Club meets, it's at my Media Arts showcase. Everyone has turned out to support me and to see Cole's film. It features members of our group talking about the loved ones they lost and about what they've found.

There's an interview with Dad that I've never seen. He glows as he talks about me, about how proud he is and about how happy he is to have met Kelsey.

Humphrey and Zelda give interviews that make the audience weep. There are even moments of humor, usually Cole doing something silly to break the ice. He's always trying to make everyone around him comfortable and happy. I realize now that he's been doing that for me for years.

When it's time to unveil my installation, I remove a sheet from over the large lit scoreboard and flip the switch. I've named the installation "The Broken Hearts Club," and it features black-and-white images with lit cutouts that tell a story. There's Humphrey with the heart on his chest, Grace with the shape of her son looking over her shoulder, Cole alone on the curb with my silhouette next to him, me down by the river with my mom's slight frame on the bench, all three lawyers holding "invisible" hearts, and Dad next to a cutout of Kelsey's profile. The last piece is my mom's note, the handwriting cut out to form words of light.

Snapshot, my love. Tell me your life story is a happy one. I'm not sad to leave. I'm filled with happiness. I was yours and you were mine. We are always connected. Take me with you, wherever you go. Take me wonderful places.

Everyone gathers around to admire the piece, and I know I've done good work. I have something to offer, and I can't wait to see what the future will bring.

Dad steps up. "I'm proud of you, honey."

"Thanks, Dad," I say. "I'm just happy to pass my class."

"I do have one comment," he says.

I'm surprised. "What's that?"

"I don't know about the title," he says. "Seems a bit…"

"Inaccurate?" offers Cole from behind me, ever the big mouth.

Dad nods. "Hmm, yes."

I turn to Cole. "Sharpie?"

He reaches into his pocket and produces one.

I grab the title placard and use the felt marker to change the title. "There," I say, placing it back. "All fixed."

Now it reads The UNBroken Hearts Club.

"Better," Dad says.

Everyone agrees. Much better.

Snapshot, Logan. Okay, Mom, a snapshot. It's summertime. I'm taking photos in color now. A lot of them are still of Cole, but that's because he's hot. I'm getting out and doing things. Living, connecting with the world, building my courage to go farther from home. Cole and I have plans to take a train tour in Europe, and I'm excited. More than that, I'm excited to feel excited.

But there's one thing I need before I leave. A new family photo. Dad, Kelsey, Cole and I go down to the river. I set up the camera to take timed photos of us all at Mom's bench.

We turn out great.

Acknowledgments

Thank you to my family for your love and support, and thank you to the fine people at Orca Book Publishers for bringing this book to life.

Brooke Carter is the author of several books for teens, including *Another Miserable Love Song* and *Learning Seventeen* in the Orca Soundings collection. She earned her MFA in creative writing at UBC and lives with her family in Maple Ridge, British Columbia. For more information, visit brookecarter.com.

9781459815537 PB

Seventeen-year-old Jane Learning is
sent to a Baptist reform school. Jane
has no interest in reforming and focuses
on plotting her next escape. But then
Hannah shows up, a gorgeous bad girl
with fiery hair and an even stormier
disposition.

orca soundings

For more information on all the books
in the Orca Soundings series, please visit
orcabook.com.

too yellow and the nail-wound blood a little too pink and applied too thick on the canvas, as if the artist thought piling on the paint would make their total lack of talent less obvious.

There is a painting of his eyes, all sad-like, over Mouse's bed.

The top of sad Jesus' head with his overgrown mullet hovers over the doorway. That one has a crown of thorns and a halo. I think either one would have been enough, but what do I know?

And then there's the one of his feet. Oh, the feet.

They look just like I always imagined God's feet would look like. Huge, wide, stubby-toed white feet in strappy brown-leather sandals with flat soles. When I first saw the painting I had to sit down on the squeaky little bed because just looking at it made me feel dizzy.

It's true, I thought. God really is a foot.

Chapter One

Intake at New Hope Academy—or, as I like to call it, No Hope—is a lot more boring than it sounds. The word *intake* seems like it might be about getting something, but really it's about taking things away. They take you away from your home, from your friends, from your old school, from your neighborhood, from sex (especially the "unholy" kind), from junk food, from television, from the sweet smell of marijuana, from staying out all night, from doing whatever you want whenever you want, from your favorite low-cut top, from your angry music, from your weird dyed hair, and from everything that makes you, well, you. After all, Baptist reform schools put a pretty heavy emphasis on the "reform" side of things.

When you walk into these unremarkable yet somehow threatening walls, they take your temperature, your medical history, your allergies, your past, your present, your future, your bad attitude, your lack of faith, and they write it all down. Oh, they love to write things down. I think they do that so they can hold your sins against you.

They want to tear you down so they can build you up fresh. I know their game. I see how it works on the others, all the sad little boys and girls who get sent here because their mommies and daddies just can't deal anymore. I see how it works on the meek little girl they pair me up with as a roommate-slash-cellmate. Marcie, her name is. Might as well be Mouse for the squeak of her voice. So timid she can't even look me in the eye.

The people here think I'm just like Mouse on the inside, a good girl waiting to get out, but their Find-Jesus program won't work on me. No, I'm a different species altogether. If Mouse is a rodent, then I'm the cat. I wonder how long it will take them to figure it out.

My stepmonster, Sheila, convinced Dad that No Hope is their last hope at straightening me out, so to speak, so they're dumping me in here along with all the other unwanted weirdo kids. Dad didn't even take time off from work to attend my "intake" and left it up to Sheila to get me settled. I guess her idea of "settled" means pushing me inside the front doors and then speeding off in her Acura.

I've been through the "orientation" process, which is really just a rundown of the rules (spoiler alert—there's a lot of them). I have a couple pairs of scratchy skirted uniforms and a blank journal, and I am now sitting here in my cell.

The room has linoleum floors and two single beds, one for me and one for Mouse, and the walls are decorated with paintings of Jesus that look like they were done by some teenager who was locked up here in the '70s or something because ol' Jesus is throwing down some sweet rock-and-roll hair. For some reason, none of the paintings show a whole-body shot. Each image is of a different part of his body. Dismembered Jesus really gives me the creeps.

Over my bed is a painting of his hands, palms up, the skin color a little too yellow and the nail-wound blood a little too pink and applied too thick on the canvas, as if the artist thought piling on the paint would make their total lack of talent less obvious.

There is a painting of his eyes, all sad-like, over Mouse's bed.

The top of sad Jesus' head with his overgrown mullet hovers over the doorway. That one has a crown of thorns and a halo. I think either one would have been enough, but what do I know?

And then there's the one of his feet. Oh, the feet.

They look just like I always imagined God's feet would look like. Huge, wide, stubby-toed white feet in strappy brown-leather sandals with flat soles. When I first saw the painting I had to sit down on the squeaky little bed because just looking at it made me feel dizzy.

It's true, I thought. God really is a foot.

orca soundings

For more information on all the books
in the Orca Soundings series, please visit
orcabook.com.